Our Three Friends Who Ate the Cookies?

Illustrated by J.-L. Macias S.

It's Christmas time. Pamela, Daniel and Nancy are so happy because the children from the nearby farm are coming to spend the holidays with them. They are all friends and go to the same school. Their names are Cathy, Diana, Mark, and their little cousin Bobby, who takes his violin everywhere he goes. The guests have brought all sorts of good things to eat. Daniel and Nancy go out to welcome their friends, but Pamela is very busy making some delicious cookies for dessert.

Soon the children go out to look for a Christmas tree for the front of the house. They want a really big, beautiful one. Daniel has an axe to cut the tree down. They also bring along two sleds which Cathy, Diana, Nancy and Bobby try to ride. Again and again they fall off the sleds, but no one is hurt. Everyone is laughing and having so much fun.

At last they find a beautiful tree. The children are so happy!
They put the tree on one of the sleds, and a big bundle of
wood on the other.

It's time to go back home. The sled rides are over for today and the children have enjoyed themselves, playing in the snow.

The children place the tree in front of the house while Pamela takes the cookies out of the oven and puts them on the windowsill to cool. Everyone must wait until after supper to eat them.

Now the children start to trim the tree. Lanterns, garlands and brightly colored paper chains the children have made themselves come out of the box and gaily decorate the tree.

Nancy and her friends decide to have a snowball fight while they wait for supper. Suddenly Pamela, looking a little angry and carrying a half-empty cookie tray, orders everyone back to the house. The children stop throwing snowballs and quietly go back to the house.

"Someone just couldn't wait for supper," says Pamela. "I see cookies are missing." Then she says, "And if you eat too many of these cookies, your hair will turn green!"

To everyone's surprise Bobby rushes to the mirror and pulls off his hat. He is so relieved to discover that his hair is not green. Of course, it was just Pamela's trick to see who stole the cookies.

Bobby promises to be good in the future, and not to be selfish and help himself before the others. Pamela suggests that they all go out and sing carols under the tree before supper. In a few minutes the children are outside playing their own musical instruments.

Bobby plays his violin. The greedy little boy who took the cookies has now become a wonderful musician. The other children are very pleased to hear how well Bobby plays. They are all quiet as they listen to him. It is a very special moment.

When Bobby has finished playing the children congratulate him.
"Oh, Bobby!" cries Nancy. "If you want to you can have my share
of the cookies. A musician like you deserves them." Everyone
laughs. It has begun to snow so they go back into the house where
a delicious supper is waiting for them. Perhaps Bobby will play his
violin again. . . .

Published in the United States and simultaneously in Canada by Joshua Morris, Inc
431 Post Road East, Westport, CT.06880
Printed in Belgium